E WONDERFUL
Wonderful you :with the Grouchy Ladybug.

For:

From:

Library of Congress Control Number: 2021948126

ISBN 978-0-06-298425-8

Book design by Rachel Zegar

22 23 24 25 26   RTLO   10 9 8 7 6 5 4 3 2 1

First Edition

Wonderful YOU

with
The Grouchy Ladybug

HARPER
An Imprint of HarperCollinsPublishers

Be
YOU.

Follow your **HEART...**

...and your IMAGINATION.

Be
SILLY.

LAUGH and smile…

…and **DANCE** for all to see.

Be
CURIOUS.

EXPLORE near and far…

…and **DISCOVER** something new.

Be
GROUCHY.

A little rain…

...makes sunny days even
BRIGHTER.

Be
GLAD.

PLAY with friends…

...and **SHARE** your gifts
with the world.

Be
PROUD
of who you are.

Celebrate
YOU.

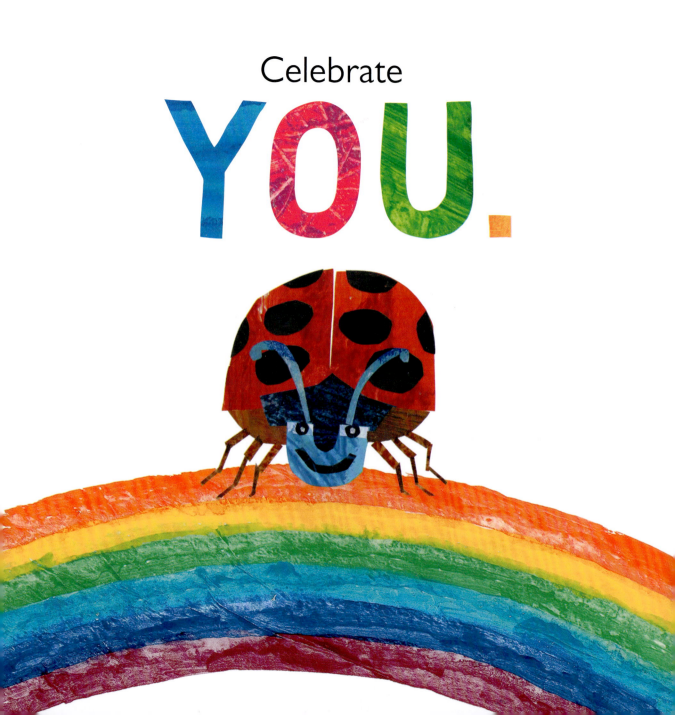

Just being you makes
the world special, too!